RAGGEDY ANDY
STORIES

RAGGEDY ANDY
STORIES
Introducing the Little Rag Brother of Raggedy Ann

Written & Illustrated by
JOHNNY GRUELLE

Macmillan Publishing Company   *New York*

Maxwell Macmillan Canada   *Toronto*

Maxwell Macmillan International
New York   Oxford   Singapore   Sydney

Publisher's Note:

Macmillan Publishing Company is proud to be reissuing this American classic in the format in which it was originally published. This reissue has been authorized by the Gruelle family, who have also provided a family memoir (see Afterword). The color illustrations have been reproduced from those in the early printings, thus restoring the delicacy and detail that were lost as the plates deteriorated over many printings. We have restored the endpapers and cover to their original conditions, and reset the text in a typeface as close in appearance as possible to the one used in the first edition. As in that edition, there are no page numbers or table of contents. The book is printed on acid-free paper for permanence, and signature-sewn in the traditional manner for ease of use.

This facsimile edition copyright © 1993 by Macmillan Publishing Company
Afterword copyright © 1993 by Kim Gruelle
All rights reserved. No part of this book may be reproduced or
transmitted in any form or by any means, electronic or
mechanical, including photocopying, recording, or by any
information storage and retrieval system, without permission in
writing from the Publisher.
Macmillan Publishing Company is part of the
Maxwell Communication
Group of Companies.
Macmillan Publishing Company
866 Third Avenue
New York, NY 10022
Maxwell Macmillan Canada, Inc.
1200 Eglinton Avenue East
Suite 200
Don Mills, Ontario M3C 3N1
Printed in the United States of America

10   9   8   7   6   5   4   3   2   1

Library of Congress Cataloging-in-Publication Data

Gruelle, Johnny, 1880?–1938.
Raggedy Andy stories : introducing the little rag brother of
Raggedy Ann / written & illustrated by Johnny Gruelle.
p.   cm.
Summary: A collection of stories that present the adventures of
the doll, Raggedy Andy, including "The Rabbit Chase," "The New Tin
Gutter," and "Doctor Raggedy Andy."
ISBN 0-02-737586-2
[1. Dolls—Fiction.] I. Title.
PZ7.G9324Rai   1993   93-21967
[E]—dc20

TO
MARCELLA'S MAMA

Gainsville, Florida,
January 8, 1919.

Johnny Gruelle,
Care of P. F. Volland Company.
Chicago, Ill.

Dear Johnny:

WHEN I saw your Raggedy Ann books and dolls in a store near here, I went right in and bought one of each, and when I had read your introduction to "Raggedy Ann" I went right up to an old trunk in my own attic and brought down the doll I am sending you with this letter.

This doll belonged to my mother and she played with it when a little girl. She treasured it highly, I know, for she kept it until I came and then she gave it to me.

The fun that we two have had together I cannot begin to tell you, but often, like the little boy who went out into the garden to eat worms when all the world seemed blue and clouded, this doll and I went out under the arbor and had our little cry together. I can still feel it's soft rag arms (as I used to imagine) about me, and hear the words of comfort (also imaginary) that were whispered in my ear.

As you say in your Raggedy Ann book, "Fairyland must be filled with rag dolls, soft loppy rag dolls who go through all the beautiful adventures found there, nestling in the crook of a dimpled arm." I truly believe there is such a fairyland

and that rag dolls were first made there, or how else could they bring so much sunshine into a child's life?

All the little girls of my acquaintance have your Raggedy Ann book and doll, and for the happiness you have brought to them let me give to you the doll of all my dolls, the doll I loved most dearly.

May it prove to you a gift from Fairyland, bringing with it all the "wish come true" that you may wish and, if possible, add to the sunshine in your life.

My mother called the doll Raggedy Andy and it was by this name that I have always known him. Is it any wonder that I was surprised when I saw the title of your book?

Introduce Raggedy Andy to Raggedy Ann, dear Johnny. Let him share in the happiness of your household.

Sincerely yours,

Raggedy Andy's "Mama."

*   *   *   *   *

Wilton, Connecticut,
January 12, 1919.

Dear John:

Your letter brings many pleasant memories to my mind and takes me back to my childhood.

Living next door to us, when I was about four years old, was a little girl named Bessie; I cannot recall her last name.

When my mother made Raggedy Ann for me, Bessie's mother made a rag doll for her, for we two always played together; as I recall, there was no fence between our two houses.

Bessie's doll was made a day or so after Raggedy Ann, I think, though I am not quite certain which of the two dolls was made first. However, Bessie's doll was given the name of Raggedy Andy, and one of the two dolls was named after the other, so that their names would sound alike.

We children played with the two rag dolls most of the time until Bessie's family moved away—when I was eight or nine years old. They had faces just alike; the mother who made the first doll probably painted both doll faces. I do not remember just how Raggedy Andy was dressed, but I know he often wore dresses over his boy clothes when Bessie and I decided that he and Raggedy Ann should be sisters for the day.

You will remember I told you about Raggedy Andy long ago, John.

Isn't it strange that the two old rag dolls should come together after all these years? I wish Raggedy Andy's "Mama" had signed her name, for I should like to write to her. Perhaps there may be some way of finding her out.

Anyway, it seems to me you have the subject for another rag doll book, for Raggedy Andy must have had some wonderful adventures in his long life.

Yours lovingly,

Mom.

*   *   *   *   *

HOW RAGGEDY ANDY CAME

ONE day Daddy took Raggedy Ann down to his office and propped her up against some books upon his desk; he wanted to have her where he could see her cheery smile all day, for, as you must surely know, smiles and happiness are truly catching.

Daddy wished to catch a whole lot of Raggedy Ann's cheeriness and happiness and put all this down on paper, so that those who did not have Raggedy Ann dolls might see just how happy and smiling a rag doll can be.

So Raggedy Ann stayed at Daddy's studio for three or four days.

She was missed very, very much at home and Marcella really longed for her, but knew that Daddy was borrowing some of Raggedy Ann's sunshine, so she did not complain.

Raggedy Ann did not complain either, for in addition to the sunny, happy smile she always wore (it was painted on), Raggedy Ann had a candy heart, and of course no one (not even a rag doll) ever complains if they have such happiness about them.

One evening, just as Daddy was finishing his day's work, a messenger boy came with a package; a nice, soft lumpy package.

Daddy opened the nice, soft lumpy package and found a letter.

Gran'ma had told Daddy, long before this, that at the time Raggedy Ann was made, a neighbor lady had made a boy doll, Raggedy Andy, for her little girl, who always played with Gran'ma.

And when Gran'ma told Daddy this she wondered whatever had become of her little playmate and the boy doll, Raggedy Andy.

After reading the letter, Daddy opened the other package which had been inside the nice, soft, lumpy package and found—Raggedy Andy.

Raggedy Andy had been carefully folded up.

His soft, loppy arms were folded up in front of him and his soft, loppy legs were folded over his soft, loppy arms, and they were held this way by a rubber band.

Raggedy Andy must have wondered why he was being "done up" this way, but it could not have caused him any worry, for in between where his feet came over his face Daddy saw his cheery smile.

After slipping off the rubber band, Daddy smoothed out the wrinkles in Raggedy Andy's arms and legs.

Then Daddy propped Raggedy Ann and Raggedy Andy up against books on his desk, so that they sat facing each other; Raggedy Ann's shoe button eyes looking straight into the shoe button eyes of Raggedy Andy.

They could not speak—not right out before a real person—so they just sat there and smiled at each other.

Daddy could not help reaching out his hands and feeling their throats.

Yes! There was a lump in Raggedy Ann's throat, and there was a lump in Raggedy Andy's throat. A cotton lump, to be sure, but a lump nevertheless.

"So, Raggedy Ann and Raggedy Andy, that is why you cannot talk, is it?" said Daddy.

"I will go away and let you have your visit to yourselves, although it is good to sit and share your happiness by watching you."

Daddy then took the rubber band and placed it around Raggedy Ann's right hand, and around Raggedy Andy's right hand, so that when he had it fixed properly they sat and held each other's hands.

Daddy knew they would wish to tell each other all the wonderful things that had happened to them since they had parted more than fifty years before.

So, locking his studio door, Daddy left the two old rag dolls looking into each other's eyes.

The next morning, when Daddy unlocked his door and looked at his desk, he saw that Raggedy Andy had fallen over so that he lay with his head in the bend of Raggedy Ann's arm.

THE NURSERY DANCE

When Raggedy Andy was first brought to the nursery he was very quiet.

Raggedy Andy did not speak all day, but he smiled pleasantly to all the other dolls. There was Raggedy Ann, the French doll, Henny, the little Dutch doll, Uncle Clem, and a few others.

Some of the dolls were without arms and legs.

One had a cracked head. She was a nice doll, though, and the others all liked her very much.

All of them had cried the night Susan (that was her name) fell off the toy box and cracked her china head.

Raggedy Andy did not speak all day.

But there was really nothing strange about this fact, after all.

None of the other dolls spoke all day, either.

Marcella had played in the nursery all day and of course they did not speak in front of her.

Marcella thought they did, though, and often had them saying things which they really were not even thinking of.

For instance, when Marcella served water with sugar in it and little oyster crackers for "tea," Raggedy Andy was thinking of Raggedy Ann, and the French doll was thinking of one time when Fido was lost.

Marcella took the French doll's hand, and passed a cup of "tea" to Raggedy Andy, and said, "Mr. Raggedy Andy, will you have another cup of tea?" as if the French doll was talking.

And then Marcella answered for Raggedy Andy, "Oh, yes, thank you! It is so delicious!"

Neither the French doll nor Raggedy Andy knew what was going on, for they were thinking real hard to themselves.

Nor did they drink the tea when it was poured for them. Marcella drank it instead.

Perhaps this was just as well, for, most of the dolls were moist inside from the "tea" of the day before.

Marcella did not always drink all of the tea, often she poured a little down their mouths.

Sugar and water, if taken in small quantities, would not give the dolls colic, Marcella would tell them, but she did not know that it made their cotton, or sawdust insides, quite sticky.

Quite often, too, Marcella forgot to wash their faces after a "tea," and Fido would do it for them when he came into the nursery and found the dolls with sweets upon their faces.

Really, Fido was quite a help in this way, but he often missed the corners of their eyes and the backs of their necks where the "tea" would run and get sticky. But he did his best and saved his little Mistress a lot of work.

No, Raggedy Andy did not speak; he merely thought a great deal.

One can, you know, when one has been a rag doll as long as Raggedy Andy had. Years and years and years and years!

Even Raggedy Ann, with all her wisdom, did not really know how long Raggedy Andy and she had been rag dolls.

If Raggedy Ann had a pencil in her rag hand and Marcella guided it for her, Raggedy Ann could count up to ten— sometimes. But why should one worry one's rag head about one's age when all one's life has been one happy experience after another, with each day filled with love and sunshine?

Raggedy Andy did not know his age, but he remembered many things that had happened years and years and years ago, when he and Raggedy Ann were quite young.

It was of these pleasant times Raggedy Andy was thinking all day, and this was the reason he did not notice that Marcella was speaking for him.

Raggedy Andy could patiently wait until Marcella put all the dollies to bed and left them for the night, alone in the nursery.

The day might have passed very slowly had it not been for the happy memories which filled Raggedy Andy's cotton-stuffed head.

But he did not even fidget.

Of course, he fell out of his chair once, and his shoe button eyes went "Click!" against the floor, but it wasn't his fault. Raggedy Andy was so loppy he could hardly be placed in a chair so that he would stay, and Marcella jiggled the table.

Marcella cried for Raggedy Andy, "AWAA! AWAA!" and picked him up and snuggled him and scolded Uncle Clem for jiggling the table.

Through all this Raggedy Andy kept right on thinking his pleasant thoughts, and really did not know he had fallen from the chair.

You see how easy it is to pass over the little bumps of life if we are happy inside.

And so Raggedy Andy was quiet all day, and so the day finally passed.

Raggedy Andy was given one of Uncle Clem's clean white nighties and shared Uncle Clem's bed. Marcella kissed them all good night and left them to sleep until morning.

But as soon as she had left the room all the dolls raised up in their beds. When their little mistress' footsteps passed out of hearing, all the dollies jumped out of their beds and gathered around Raggedy Andy.

Raggedy Ann introduced them one by one and Raggedy Andy shook hands with each.

"I am very happy to know you all!" he said, in a voice as kindly as Raggedy Ann's, "and I hope we will all like each other as much as Raggedy Ann and I have always liked each other!"

"Oh, indeed we shall!" the dollies all answered. "We love Raggedy Ann because she is so kindly and happy, and we know we shall like you too, for you talk like Raggedy Ann and have the same cheery smile!"

"Now that we know each other so well, what do you say to a game, Uncle Clem?" Raggedy Andy cried, as he caught Uncle Clem and danced about the floor.

Henny, the Dutch doll, dragged the little square music box out into the center of the room and wound it up. Then all, catching hands, danced in a circle around it, laughing and shouting in their tiny doll voices.

"That was lots of fun!" Raggedy Andy said, when the music stopped and all the dolls had taken seats upon the floor facing him. "You know I have been shut up in a trunk up in an attic for years and years and years."

"Wasn't it very lonesome in the trunk all that time?"

Susan asked in her queer little cracked voice. You see, her head had been cracked.

"Oh, not at all," Raggedy Andy replied, "for there was always a nest of mice down in the corner of the trunk. Cute little Mama and Daddy mice, and lots of little teeny weeny baby mice. And when the mama and daddy mice were away, I used to cuddle the tiny little baby mice!"

"No wonder you were never lonesome!" said Uncle Clem, who was very kind and loved everybody and everything.

"No, I was never lonesome in the old trunk in the attic, but it is far more pleasant to be out again and living here with all you nice friends!" said Raggedy Andy.

And all the dolls thought so too, for already they loved Raggedy Andy's happy smile and knew he would prove to be as kindly and lovable as Raggedy Ann.

JOHNNY GRUELLE

THE SPINNING WHEEL

One night, after all the household had settled down to sleep, Raggedy Andy sat up in bed and tickled Uncle Clem.

Uncle Clem twisted and wiggled in his sleep until finally he could stand it no longer and awakened.

"I dreamed that some one told me the funniest story!" said Uncle Clem; "But I cannot remember what it was!"

"I was tickling you!" laughed Raggedy Andy.

When the other dolls in the nursery heard Raggedy Andy and Uncle Clem talking, they too sat up in their beds.

"We've been so quiet all day," said Raggedy Andy. "Let's have a good romp!"

This suggestion suited all the dolls, so they jumped out of their beds and ran over towards Raggedy Andy's and Uncle Clem's little bed.

Raggedy Andy, always in for fun, threw his pillow at Henny, the Dutch doll.

Henny did not see the pillow coming towards him so he was knocked head over heels.

Henny always said "Mama" when he was tilted backward or forward, and when the pillow rolled him over and over, he cried, "Mama, Mama, Mama!"

It was not because it hurt him, for you know Santa Claus always sees to it that each doll he makes in his great workshop is covered with a very magical Wish, and this Wish always keeps them from getting hurt.

Henny could talk just as well as any of the other dolls when he was standing up, sitting, or lying down, but if he was being tipped forward and backward, all he could say was, "Mama."

This amused Henny as much as it did the other dolls, so when he jumped to his feet he laughed and threw the pillow back at Raggedy Andy.

Raggedy Andy tried to jump to one side, but forgot that he was on the bed, and he and Uncle Clem went tumbling to the floor.

Then all the dolls ran to their beds and brought their pillows and had the jolliest pillow fight imaginable.

The excitement ran so high and the pillows flew so fast, the floor of the nursery was soon covered with feathers. It was only when all the dolls had stopped to rest and put the feathers back into the pillow cases that Raggedy Andy discovered he had lost one of his arms in the scuffle.

The dolls were worried over this and asked, "What will Marcella say when she sees that Raggedy Andy has lost an arm?"

"We can push it up his sleeve!" said Uncle Clem. "Then when Raggedy Andy is taken out of bed in the morning, Marcella will find his arm is loose!"

"It has been hanging by one or two threads for a day or more!" said Raggedy Andy. "I noticed the other day that sometimes my thumb was turned clear around to the back, and I knew then that the arm was hanging by one or two threads and the threads were twisted."

Uncle Clem pushed Raggedy Andy's arm up through his sleeve, but every time Raggedy Andy jumped about, he lost his arm again.

"This will never do!" said Raggedy Ann. "Raggedy Andy is lopsided with only one arm and he cannot join in our games as well as if he had two arms!"

"Oh, I don't mind that!" laughed Raggedy Andy. "Mar-

cella will sew it on in the morning and I will be all right, I'm sure!"

"Perhaps Raggedy Ann can sew it on now!" suggested Uncle Clem.

"Yes, Raggedy Ann can sew it on!" all the dolls cried. "She can play Peter, Peter, Pumpkin Eater on the toy piano and she can sew!"

"I will gladly try," said Raggedy Ann, "but there are no needles or thread in the nursery, and I have to have a thimble so the needle can be pressed through Raggedy Andy's cloth!"

"Marcella always gets a needle from Mama!" said the French Doll.

"I know," said Raggedy Ann, "but we cannot waken Mama to ask her!"

The dolls all laughed at this, for they knew very well that even had Mama been awake, they would not have asked her for needle and thread, because they did not wish her to know they could act and talk just like real people.

"Perhaps we can get the things out of the machine drawer!" Henny suggested.

"Yes," cried Susan, "let's all go get the things out of the machine drawer! Come on, everybody!"

And Susan, although she had only a cracked head, ran out the nursery door followed by all the rest of the dolls.

Even the tiny little penny dolls clicked their china heels upon the floor as they followed the rest, and Raggedy Andy, carrying his loose arm, thumped along in the rear.

Raggedy Andy had not lived in the house as long as the others; so he did not know the way to the room in which the machine stood.

After much climbing and pulling, the needle and thread and thimble were taken from the drawer, and all raced back again to the nursery.

Uncle Clem took off Raggedy Andy's waist, and the other dolls all sat around watching while Raggedy Ann sewed the arm on again.

Raggedy Ann had only taken two stitches when she began laughing so hard she had to quit. Of course when Raggedy Ann laughed, all the other dolls laughed too, for laughter, like yawning, is very catching.

"I was just thinking!" said Raggedy Ann. "Remember, 'way, 'way back, a long, long time ago, I sewed this arm on once before?" she asked Raggedy Andy.

"I do remember, now that you mention it," said Raggedy Andy, "but I can not remember how the arm came off!"

"Tell us about it!" all the dolls cried.

"Let's see!" Raggedy Ann began. "Your Mistress left you over at our house one night, and after everyone had gone to bed, we went up into the attic!"

"Oh, yes! I do remember now!" Raggedy Andy laughed. "We played with the large whirligig!"

"Yes," Raggedy Ann said. "The large spinning wheel. We held on to the wheel and went round and round! And when we were having the most fun, your feet got fastened between the wheel and the rod which held the wheel in position and there you hung, head down!"

"I remember, you were working the pedal and I was sailing around very fast," said Raggedy Andy, "and all of a sudden the wheel stopped!"

"We would have laughed at the time," Raggedy Ann explained to the other dolls, "but you see it was quite serious."

"My mistress had put us both to bed for the night, and if she had discovered us 'way up in the attic, she would have wondered how in the world we got there! So there was nothing to do but get Raggedy Andy out of the tangle!"

"But you pulled me out all right!" Raggedy Andy laughed.

"Yes, I pulled and I pulled until I pulled one of Raggedy Andy's arms off," Raggedy Ann said. "And then I pulled and pulled until finally his feet came out of the wheel and we both tumbled to the floor!"

"Then we ran downstairs as fast as we could and climbed into bed, didn't we!" Raggedy Andy laughed.

"Yes, we did!" Raggedy Ann replied. "And when we jumped into bed, we remembered that we had left Raggedy Andy's arm lying up on the attic floor, so we had to run back up there and get it! Remember, Raggedy Andy?"

"Yes! Wasn't it lots of fun?"

"Indeed it was!" Raggedy Ann agreed.

"Raggedy Andy wanted to let the arm remain off until the next morning, but I decided it would be better to have it sewed on, just as it had been when Mistress put us to bed. So, just like tonight, we went to the pincushion and found a needle and thread and I sewed it on for him!"

"There!" Raggedy Ann said, as she wound the thread around her hand and pulled, so that the thread broke near Raggedy Andy's shoulder. "It's sewed on again, good as new!"

"Thank you, Raggedy Ann!" said Raggedy Andy, as he threw the arm about Raggedy Ann's neck and gave her a hug.

"Now we can have another game!" Uncle Clem cried as he helped Raggedy Andy into his waist and buttoned it for him.

Just then the little Cuckoo Clock on the nursery wall went, "Whirrr!" the little door opened, and the little bird put out his head and cried, "Cuckoo! cuckoo! cuckoo! cuckoo!"

"No more games!" Raggedy Ann said. "We must be very quiet from now on. The folks will be getting up soon!"

"Last one in bed is a monkey!" cried Raggedy Andy.

There was a wild scramble as the dolls rushed for their beds, and Susan, having to be careful of her cracked head, was the monkey. So Raggedy Andy, seeing that Susan was slow about getting into her bed, jumped out and helped her.

Then, climbing into the little bed which Uncle Clem shared with him, he pulled the covers up to his eyes and, after pretending to snore a couple of times, he lay very quiet, thinking of the kindness of his doll friends about him, until Marcella came and took him down to breakfast.

And all the other dolls smiled at him as he left the room, for they were very happy to know that their little mistress loved him as much as they did.

JOHNNY GRUELLE

THE TAFFY PULL

"I know how we can have a whole lot of fun!" Raggedy Andy said to the other dolls. "We'll have a taffy pull!"

"Do you mean crack the whip, Raggedy Andy?" asked the French doll.

"He means a tug of war, don't you, Raggedy Andy?" asked Henny.

"No," Raggedy Andy replied, "I mean a taffy pull!"

"If it's lots of fun, then show us how to play the game!" Uncle Clem said. "We like to have fun, don't we?" And Uncle Clem turned to all the other dolls as he asked the question.

"It really is not a game," Raggedy Andy explained. "You see, it is only a taffy pull.

"We take sugar and water and butter and a little vinegar and put it all on the stove to cook. When it has cooked until it strings 'way out when you dip some up in a spoon, or gets hard when you drop some of it in a cup of water, then it is candy.

"Then it must be placed upon buttered plates until it has cooled a little, and then each one takes some of the candy and pulls and pulls until it gets real white. Then it is called 'Taffy'."

"That will be loads of fun!" "Show us how to begin!"

"Let's have a taffy pull!" "Come on, everybody!" the dolls cried.

"Just one moment!" Raggedy Ann said. She had remained quiet before, for she had been thinking very hard, so hard, in fact, that two stitches had burst in the back of her rag head. The dolls, in their eagerness to have the taffy pull, were dancing about Raggedy Andy, but when Raggedy Ann spoke, in her soft cottony voice, they all quieted down and waited for her to speak again.

"I was just thinking," Raggedy Ann said, "that it would be very nice to have the taffy pull, but suppose some of the folks smell the candy while it is cooking."

"There is no one at home!" Raggedy Andy said. "I thought of that, Raggedy Ann. They have all gone over to Cousin Jenny's house and will not be back until day after tomorrow. I heard Mama tell Marcella."

"If that is the case, we can have the taffy pull and all the fun that goes with it!" Raggedy Ann cried, as she started for the nursery door.

After her ran all the dollies, their little feet pitter-patting across the floor and down the hall.

When they came to the stairway Raggedy Ann, Raggedy Andy, Uncle Clem and Henny threw themselves down the stairs, turning over and over as they fell.

The other dolls, having china heads, had to be much more careful; so they slid down the banisters, or jumped from one step to another.

Raggedy Ann, Raggedy Andy, Uncle Clem and Henny piled in a heap at the bottom of the steps, and by the time they had untangled themselves and helped each other up, the other dolls were down the stairs.

To the kitchen they all raced. There they found the fire in the stove still burning.

Raggedy Andy brought a small stew kettle, while the others brought the sugar and water and a large spoon. They could not find the vinegar and decided not to use it, anyway.

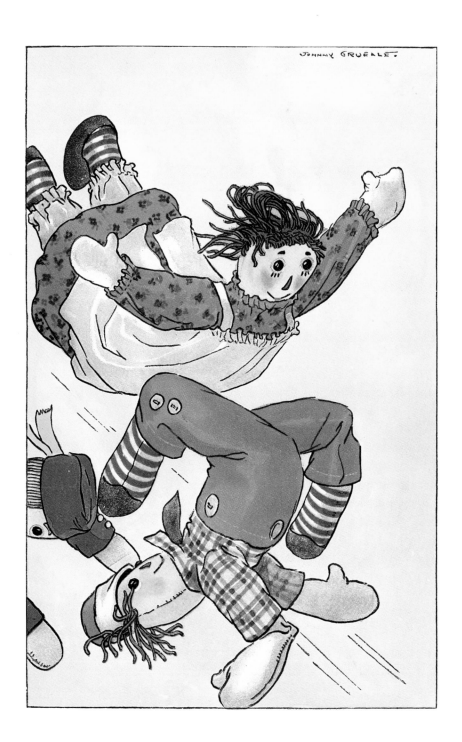

Raggedy Andy stood upon the stove and watched the candy, dipping into it every once in a while to see if it had cooked long enough, and stirring it with the large spoon.

At last the candy began to string out from the spoon when it was held above the stew kettle, and after trying a few drops in a cup of cold water, Raggedy Andy pronounced it "done."

Uncle Clem pulled out a large platter from the pantry, and Raggedy Ann dipped her rag hand into the butter jar and buttered the platter.

The candy, when it was poured into the platter, was a lovely golden color and smelled delicious to the dolls. Henny could not wait until it cooled; so he put one of his chamois skin hands into the hot candy.

Of course it did not burn Henny, but when he pulled his hand out again, it was covered with a great ball of candy, which strung out all over the kitchen floor and got upon his clothes.

Then too, the candy cooled quickly, and in a very short time Henny's hand was encased in a hard ball of candy. Henny couldn't wiggle any of his fingers on that hand and he was sorry he had been so hasty.

While waiting for the candy to cool, Raggedy Andy said, "We must rub butter upon our hands before we pull the candy, or else it will stick to our hands as it has done to Henny's hands and have to wear off!"

"Will this hard ball of candy have to wear off of my hand?" Henny asked. "It is so hard, I cannot wiggle any of my fingers!"

"It will either have to wear off, or you will have to soak your hand in water for a long time, until the candy on it melts!" said Raggedy Andy.

"Dear me!" said Henny.

Uncle Clem brought the poker then and, asking Henny to put his hand upon the stove leg, he gave the hard candy a few sharp taps with the poker and chipped the candy from Henny's hand.

"Thank you, Uncle Clem!" Henny said, as he wiggled his fingers. "That feels much better!"

Raggedy Andy told all the dolls to rub butter upon their hands.

"The candy is getting cool enough to pull!" he said.

Then, when all the dolls had their hands nice and buttery, Raggedy Andy cut them each a nice piece of candy and showed them how to pull it.

"Take it in one hand this way," he said, "and pull it with the other hand, like this!"

When all the dolls were supplied with candy they sat about and pulled it, watching it grow whiter and more silvery the longer they pulled.

Then, when the taffy was real white, it began to grow harder and harder, so the smaller dolls could scarcely pull it any more.

When this happened, Raggedy Andy, Raggedy Ann, Uncle Clem and Henny, who were larger, took the little dolls' candy and mixed it with what they had been pulling until all the taffy was snow white.

Then Raggedy Andy pulled it out into a long rope and held it while Uncle Clem hit the ends a sharp tap with the edge of the spoon.

This snipped the taffy into small pieces, just as easily as you might break icicles with a few sharp taps of a stick.

The small pieces of white taffy were placed upon the buttered platter again and the dolls all danced about it, singing and laughing, for this had been the most fun they had had for a long, long time.

"But what shall we do with it?" Raggedy Ann asked.

"Yes, what shall we do with it!" Uncle Clem said. "We can't let it remain in the platter here upon the kitchen floor! We must hide it, or do something with it!"

"While we are trying to think of a way to dispose of it, let us be washing the stew kettle and the spoon!" said practical Raggedy Ann.

"That is a very happy thought, Raggedy Ann!" said Raggedy Andy. "For it will clean the butter and candy from our hands while we are doing it!"

So the stew kettle was dragged to the sink and filled with water, the dolls all taking turns scraping the candy from the sides of the kettle, and scrubbing the inside with a cloth.

When the kettle was nice and clean and had been wiped dry, Raggedy Andy found a roll of waxed paper in the pantry upon one of the shelves.

"We'll wrap each piece of taffy in a nice little piece of paper," he said, "then we'll find a nice paper bag, and put all the pieces inside the bag, and throw it from the upstairs window when someone passes the house so that someone may have the candy!"

All the dolls gathered about the platter on the floor, and while Raggedy Andy cut the paper into neat squares, the dolls wrapped the taffy in the papers.

Then the taffy was put into a large bag, and with much pulling and tugging it was finally dragged up into the nursery, where a window faced out toward the street.

Then, just as a little boy and a little girl, who looked as though they did not ever have much candy, passed the house, the dolls all gave a push and sent the bag tumbling to the sidewalk.

The two children laughed and shouted, "Thank you," when they saw that the bag contained candy, and the dolls, peeping from behind the lace curtains, watched the two happy faced children eating the taffy as they skipped down the street.

When the children had passed out of sight, the dolls climbed down from the window.

"That was lots of fun!" said the French doll, as she smoothed her skirts and sat down beside Raggedy Andy.

"I believe Raggedy Andy must have a candy heart too, like Raggedy Ann!" said Uncle Clem.

"No!" Raggedy Andy answered, "I'm just stuffed with white cotton and I have no candy heart, but some day perhaps I shall have!"

"A candy heart is very nice!" Raggedy Ann said. (You know, she had one.) "But one can be just as nice and happy and full of sunshine without a candy heart."

"I almost forgot to tell you," said Raggedy Andy, "that when pieces of taffy are wrapped in little pieces of paper, just as we wrapped them, they are called 'Kisses'."

THE RABBIT CHASE

"Well, what shall we play tonight?" asked Henny, the Dutch doll, when the house was quiet and the dolls all knew that no one else was awake.

Raggedy Andy was just about to suggest a good game, when Fido, who sometimes slept in a basket in the nursery, growled.

All the dollies looked in his direction.

Fido was standing up with his ears sticking as straight in the air as loppy silken puppy dog ears can stick up.

"He must have been dreaming!" said Raggedy Andy.

"No, I wasn't dreaming!" Fido answered. "I heard something go, 'Scratch! Scratch!' as plain as I hear you!"

"Where did the sound come from, Fido?" Raggedy Andy asked when he saw that Fido really was wide awake.

"From outside somewhere!" Fido answered. "And if I could get out without disturbing all the folks, I'd run out and see what it might be! Perhaps I had better bark!"

"Please do not bark!" Raggedy Andy cried as he put his rag arm around Fido's nose. "You will awaken everybody in the house. We can open a door or a window for you and let you out, if you must go!"

"I wish you would. Listen! There it is again: 'Scratch! Scratch!' What can it be?"

"You may soon see!" said Raggedy Andy. "We'll let you out, but please don't sit at the door and bark and bark to get back in again, as you usually do, for we are going to play a good game and we may not hear you!"

"You can sleep out in the shed after you have found out what it is," said Raggedy Andy.

As soon as the dolls opened the door for Fido, he went running across the lawn, barking in a loud shrill voice. He ran down behind the shed and through the garden, and then back towards the house again.

Raggedy Andy and Uncle Clem stood looking out of the door, the rest of the dolls peeping over their shoulders, so when something came jumping through the door, it hit Uncle Clem and Raggedy Andy and sent them flying against the other dolls behind them.

All the dolls went down in a wiggling heap on the floor.

It was surprising that the noise and confusion did not waken Daddy and the rest of the folks, for just as the dolls were untangling themselves from each other and getting upon their feet, Fido came jumping through the door and sent the dolls tumbling again.

Fido quit barking when he came through the door.

"Which way did he go?" he asked, when he could get his breath.

"What was it?" Raggedy Andy asked in return.

"It was a rabbit!" Fido cried. "He ran right in here, for I could smell his tracks!"

"We could feel him!" Raggedy Andy laughed.

"I could not tell you which way he went!" Uncle Clem said, "Except I feel sure he came through the door and into the house!"

None of the dolls knew into which room the rabbit had run.

Finally, after much sniffing, Fido traced the rabbit to the nursery, where, when the dolls followed, they saw the rabbit crouching behind the rocking horse.

Fido whined and cried because he could not get to the rabbit and bite him.

"You should be ashamed of yourself, Fido!" cried Raggedy Ann. "Just see how the poor bunny is trembling!"

"He should not come scratching around our house if he doesn't care to be chased!" said Fido.

"Why don't you stay out in the woods and fields where you really belong?" Raggedy Andy asked the rabbit.

"I came to leave some Easter eggs!" the bunny answered in a queer little quavery voice.

"An Easter bunny!" all the dolls cried, jumping about and clapping their hands. "An Easter bunny!"

"Well!" was all Fido could say, as he sat down and began wagging his tail.

"You may come out from behind the rocking horse now, Easter bunny!" said Raggedy Andy. "Fido will not hurt you, now that he knows, will you, Fido?"

"Indeed I won't!" Fido replied. "I'm sorry that I chased you! And I remember now, I had to jump over a basket out by the shed! Was that yours?"

"Yes, it was full of Easter eggs and colored grasses for the little girl who lives here!" the bunny said.

When the Easter bunny found out that Fido and the dolls were his friends, he came out from behind the rocking horse and hopped across the floor to the door.

"I must go see if any of the eggs are broken, for if they are, I will have to run home and color some more! I was just about to make a nice nest and put the eggs in it when Fido came bouncing out at me!"

And with a squeeky little laugh the Easter bunny, followed by Fido and all the dolls, hopped across the lawn towards the shed. There they found the basket. Four of the lovely colored Easter eggs were broken.

"I will run home and color four more. It will only take a few minutes, so when I return and scratch again to make a nest, please do not bark at me!" said the Easter bunny.

"I won't! I promise!" Fido laughed.

"May we go with you and watch you color the Easter eggs?" Raggedy Andy begged.

"Indeed you may!" the Easter bunny answered. "Can you run fast?"

Then down through the garden and out through a crack in the fence the Easter bunny hopped, with a long string of dolls trailing behind.

When they came to the Easter bunny's home, they found Mama Easter bunny and a lot of little teeny weeny bunnies who would some day grow up to be big Easter bunnies like their Mama and Daddy bunny.

The Easter bunny told them of his adventure with Fido, and all joined in his laughter when they found it had turned out well at the end.

The Easter bunny put four eggs on to boil and while these were boiling he mixed up a lot of pretty colors.

When the eggs were boiled, he dipped the four eggs into the pretty colored dye and then painted lovely flowers on them.

When the Easter bunny had finished painting the eggs he put them in his basket and, with all the dolls running along beside him, they returned to the house.

"Why not make the nest right in the nursery?" Raggedy Andy asked.

"That would be just the thing! Then the little girl would wonder and wonder how I could ever get into the nursery without awakening the rest of the folks, for she will never suspect that you dolls and Fido let me in!"

So with Raggedy Andy leading the way, they ran up to the nursery and there, 'way back in a corner, they watched the Easter bunny make a lovely nest and put the Easter eggs in it.

And in the morning when Marcella came in to see the dolls you can imagine her surprise when she found the pretty gift of the Easter bunny.

"How in the world did the bunny get inside the house and into this room without awakening Fido?" she laughed.

And Fido, pretending to be asleep, slowly opened one eye and winked over the edge of his basket at Raggedy Andy.

And Raggedy Andy smiled back at Fido, but never said a word.

JOHNNY GRUELLE

THE NEW TIN GUTTER

All day Saturday the men had worked out upon the eaves of the house and the dolls facing the window could see them.

The men made quite a lot of noise with their hammers, for they were putting new gutters around the eaves, and pounding upon tin makes a great deal of noise.

Marcella had not played with the dolls all that day, for she had gone visiting; so when the men hammered and made a lot of noise, the dolls could talk to each other without fear of anyone hearing or knowing they were really talking to each other.

"What are they doing now?" Raggedy Andy asked.

He was lying with his head beneath a little bed quilt, just as Marcella had dropped him when she left the nursery; so he could not see what was going on.

"We can only see the men's legs as they pass the window," answered Uncle Clem. "But they are putting new shingles or something on the roof!"

After the men had left their work and gone home to supper and the house was quiet, Raggedy Andy cautiously moved his head out from under the little bed quilt and, seeing that the coast was clear, sat up.

This was a signal for all the dolls to sit up and smooth out the wrinkles in their clothes.

The nursery window was open; so Raggedy Andy lifted the penny dolls to the sill and climbed up beside them.

Leaning out, he could look along the new shiny tin gutter the men had put in place.

"Here's a grand place to have a lovely slide!" he said as he gave one of the penny dolls a scoot down the shiny tin gutter.

"Whee! See her go!" Raggedy Andy cried.

All the other dolls climbed upon the window sill beside him.

"Scoot me too!" cried the other little penny doll in her squeeky little voice, and Raggedy Andy took her in his rag hand and gave her a great swing which sent her scooting down the shiny tin gutter, "Kerswish!"

Then Raggedy Andy climbed into the gutter himself and, taking a few steps, spread out his feet and went scooting down the shiny tin.

The other dolls followed his example and scooted along behind him.

When Raggedy Andy came to the place where he expected to find the penny dolls lying, they were nowhere about.

"Perhaps you scooted them farther than you thought!" Uncle Clem said.

"Perhaps I did!" Raggedy Andy said, "We will look around the bend in the eave!"

"Oh dear!" he exclaimed when he had peeped around the corner of the roof, "the gutter ends here and there is nothing but a hole!"

"They must have scooted right into the hole," Henny, the Dutch doll said.

Raggedy Andy lay flat upon the shiny tin and looked down into the hole.

"Are you down there, penny dolls?" he called.

There was no answer.

"I hope their heads were not broken!" Raggedy Ann said.

"I'm so sorry I scooted them!" Raggedy Andy cried, as he brushed his hand over his shoe button eyes.

"Maybe if you hold to my feet, I can reach down the hole and find them and pull them up again!" he added.

Uncle Clem and Henny each caught hold of a foot of Raggedy Andy and let him slide down into the hole.

It was a rather tight fit, but Raggedy Andy wiggled and twisted until all the dolls could see of him were his two feet.

"I can't find them!" he said in muffled tones. "Let me down farther and I think I'll be able to reach them!"

Now Henny and Uncle Clem thought that Raggedy Andy meant for them to let go of his feet and this they did.

Raggedy Andy kept wiggling and twisting until he came to a bend in the pipe and could go no farther.

"I can't find them!" he cried. "They have gone farther down the pipe! Now you can pull me up!"

"We can't reach you, Raggedy Andy!" Uncle Clem called down the pipe. "Try to wiggle back up a piece and we will catch your feet and pull you up!"

Raggedy Andy tried to wiggle backward up the pipe, but his clothes caught upon a little piece of tin which stuck out from the inside of the pipe and there he stayed. He could neither go down nor come back up.

"What shall we do?" Uncle Clem cried, "The folks will never find him down there, for we can not tell them where he is, and they will never guess it!"

The dolls were all very sad. They stayed out upon the shiny new tin gutter until it began raining and hoped and hoped that Raggedy Andy could get back up to them.

Then they went inside the nursery and sat looking out the window until it was time for the folks to get up and the house to be astir. Then they went back to the position each had been in, when Marcella had left them.

And although they were very quiet, each one was so sorry to lose Raggedy Andy, and each felt that he would never be found again.

"The rain must have soaked his cotton through and through!" sighed Raggedy Ann. "For all the water from the house runs down the shiny tin gutters and down the pipe into a rain barrel at the bottom!"

Then Raggedy Ann remembered that there was an opening at the bottom of the pipe.

"Tomorrow night if we have a chance, we dolls must take a stick and see if we can reach Raggedy Andy from the bottom of the pipe and pull him down to us!" she thought.

Marcella came up to the nursery and played all day, watching the rain patter upon the new tin gutter. She wondered where Raggedy Andy was, although she did not get worried about him until she had asked Mama where he might be.

"He must be just where you left him!" Mama said.

"I cannot remember where I left him!" Marcella said.

"I thought he was with all the other dolls in the nursery, though!"

All day Sunday it rained and all of Sunday night, and Monday morning when Daddy started to work it was still raining.

As Daddy walked out of the front gate, he turned to wave good-bye to Mama and Marcella and then he saw something.

Daddy came right back into the house and called up the men who had put in the new shiny tin gutters.

"The drain pipe is plugged up. Some of you must have left shavings or something in the eaves, and it has washed down into the pipe, so that the water pours over the gutter in sheets!"

"We will send a man right up to fix it!" the men said.

So along about ten o'clock that morning one of the men came to fix the pipe.

But although he punched a long pole down the pipe, and punched and punched, he could not dislodge whatever it was which plugged the pipe and kept the water from running through it.

Johnny Gruelle

Then the man measured with his stick, so that he knew just where the place was, and with a pair of tin shears he cut a section from the pipe and found Raggedy Andy.

Raggedy Andy was punched quite out of shape and all jammed together, but when the man straightened out the funny little figure, Raggedy Andy looked up at him with his customary happy smile.

The man laughed and carried little water-soaked Raggedy Andy into the house.

"I guess your little girl must have dropped this rag doll down into the drain pipe!" the man said to Mama.

"I'm so glad you found him!" Mama said to the man.

"We have hunted all over the house for him! Marcella could not remember where she put him; so when I get him nice and dry, I'll hide him in a nice easy place for her to find, and she will not know he has been out in the rain all night!"

So Mama put Raggedy Andy behind the radiator and there he sat all afternoon, steaming and drying out.

And as he sat there he smiled and smiled, even though there was no one to see him.

He felt very happy within and he liked to smile, anyway, because his smile was painted on.

And another reason Raggedy Andy smiled was because he was not lonesome.

Inside his waist were the two little penny dolls.

The man had punched Raggedy Andy farther down into the pipe, and he had been able to reach the two little dolls and tuck them into a safe place.

"Won't they all be surprised to see us back again!" Raggedy Andy whispered as he patted the two little penny dolls with his soft rag hands.

And the two little penny dolls nestled against Raggedy Andy's soft cotton stuffed body, and thought how nice it was to have such a happy, sunny friend.

DOCTOR RAGGEDY ANDY

Raggedy Andy, Raggedy Ann, Uncle Clem and Henny were not given medicine.

Because, you see, they had no mouths.

That is, mouths through which medicine could be poured.

Their mouths were either painted on, or were sewed on with yarn.

Sometimes the medicine spoon would be touched to their faces but none of the liquid be given them. Except accidentally.

But the French doll had a lovely mouth for taking medicine; it was open and showed her teeth in a dimpling smile.

She also had soft brown eyes which opened and closed when she was tilted backward or forward.

The medicine which was given the dolls had great curing properties.

It would cure the most stubborn case of croup, measles, whooping cough or any other ailment the dolls had wished upon them by their little Mistress.

Some days all the dolls would be put to bed with "measles" but in the course of half an hour they would have every other ailment in the Doctor book.

The dolls enjoyed it very much, for, you see, Marcella always tried the medicine first to see if it was strong enough before she gave any to the dolls.

So the dolls really did not get as much of the medicine as their little mistress.

The wonderful remedy was made from a very old recipe handed down from ancient times.

This recipe is guaranteed to cure every ill a doll may have.

The medicine was made from brown sugar and water. Perhaps you may have used it for your dollies.

The medicine was also used as "tea" and "soda water," except when the dolls were supposed to be ill.

Having nothing but painted or yarn mouths, the ailments of Raggedy Andy, Raggedy Ann, Uncle Clem and Henny, the Dutch doll, mostly consisted of sprained wrists, arms and legs, or perhaps a headache and a toothache.

None of them knew they had the trouble until Marcella had wrapped up the "injured" rag arm, leg or head, and had explained in detail just what was the matter.

Raggedy Andy, Raggedy Ann, Uncle Clem, or Henny were just as happy with their heads tied up for the toothache as they were without their heads tied up.

Not having teeth, naturally they could not have the tooth-ache, and if they could furnish amusement for Marcella by having her pretend they had the toothache, then that made them very happy.

So this day, the French doll was quite ill. She started out with the "croup," and went through the "measles," "whooping cough," and "yellow fever" in an hour.

The attack came on quite suddenly.

The French doll was sitting quietly in one of the little red chairs, smiling the prettiest of dimpling smiles at Raggedy Andy, and thinking of the romp the dolls would have that night after the house grew quiet, when Marcella discovered that the French doll had the "croup" and put her to bed.

The French doll closed her eyes when put to bed, but the rest of her face did not change expression. She still wore her happy smile.

Marcella mixed the medicine very "strong" and poured it into the French doll's open mouth.

She was given a "dose" every minute or so.

It was during the "yellow fever" stage that Marcella was called to supper and left the dolls in the nursery alone.

Marcella did not play with them again that evening; so the dolls all remained in the same position until Marcella and the rest of the folks went to bed.

Then Raggedy Andy jumped from his chair and wound up the little music box. "Let's start with a lively dance!" he cried.

When the music started tinkling he caught the French doll's hand, and danced 'way across the nursery floor before he discovered that her soft brown eyes remained closed as they were when she lay upon the "sick" bed.

All the dolls gathered around Raggedy Andy and the French doll.

"I can't open my eyes!" she said.

Raggedy Andy tried to open the French doll's eyes with his soft rag hands, but it was no use.

They shook her. This sometimes has the desired effect when dolls do not open their eyes.

They shook her again and again. It was no use, her eyes remained closed.

"It must be the sticky, sugary 'medicine'!" said Uncle Clem.

"I really believe it must be!" the French doll replied. "The 'medicine' seemed to settle in the back of my head when I was lying down, and I can still feel it back there!"

"That must be it, and now it has hardened and keeps your pretty eyes from working!" said Raggedy Ann. "What shall we do?"

Raggedy Andy and Raggedy Ann walked over to a corner of the nursery and thought and thought. They pulled their foreheads down into wrinkles with their hands, so that they might think harder.

JOHNNY GRUELLE.

Finally Raggedy Ann cried, "I've thought of a plan!" and went skipping from the corner out to where the other dolls sat about the French doll.

"We must stand her upon her head, then the 'medicine' will run up into her hair, for there is a hole in the top of her head. I remember seeing it when her hair came off one time!"

"No sooner said than done!" cried Uncle Clem, as he took the French doll by the waist and stood her upon her head.

"That should be long enough!" Raggedy Ann said, when Uncle Clem had held the French doll in this position for five minutes.

But when the French doll was again placed upon her feet her eyes still remained tightly closed.

All this time, Raggedy Andy had remained in the corner, thinking as hard as his rag head would think.

He thought and thought, until the yarn hair upon his head stood up in the air and wiggled.

"If the 'medicine' did not run up into her hair when she stood upon her head," thought Raggedy Andy, "then it is because the 'medicine' could not run; so, if the medicine can not run, it is because it is too sticky and thick to run out the hole in the top of her head." He also thought a lot more.

At last he turned to the others and said out loud, "I can't seem to think of a single way to help her open her eyes unless we take off her hair and wash the medicine from inside her china head."

"Why didn't I think of that?" Raggedy Ann asked. "That is just the way we shall have to do!"

So Raggedy Ann caught hold of the French doll's feet, and Raggedy Andy caught hold of the French doll's lively curls, and they pulled and they pulled.

Then the other dolls caught hold of Raggedy Ann and Raggedy Andy and pulled and pulled, until finally, with a sharp "R-R-Rip!" the French doll's hair came off, and the dolls who were pulling went tumbling over backwards.

JOHNNY GRUELLE.

Laughingly they scrambled to their feet and sat the French doll up, so they might look into the hole in the top of her head.

Yes, the sticky "medicine" had grown hard and would not let the French doll's eyes open.

Raggedy Andy put his hand inside and pushed on the eyes so that they opened.

This was all right, only now the eyes would not close when the French doll lay down. She tried it.

So Raggedy Andy ran down into the kitchen and brought up a small tin cup full of warm water and a tiny rag.

With these he loosened the sticky "medicine" and washed the inside of the French doll's head nice and clean.

There were lots of cooky and cracker crumbs inside her head, too.

Raggedy Andy washed it all nice and clean, and then wet the glue which made the pretty curls stay on.

So when her hair was placed upon her head again, the French doll was as good as new.

"Thank you all very much!" she said, as she tilted backwards and forwards, and found that her eyes worked very easily.

Raggedy Andy again wound up the little music box and, catching the French doll about the waist, started a rollicking dance which lasted until the roosters in the neighborhood began their morning crowing.

Then, knowing the folks might soon be astir, the dolls left off their playing, and all took the same positions they had been in when Marcella left them the night before.

And so Marcella found them.

The French doll was in bed with her eyes closed, and her happy dimpling smile lighting up her pretty face.

And to this day, the dollies' little mistress does not know that Raggedy Andy was the doctor who cured the French doll of her only ill.

JOHNNY GRUELLE

RAGGEDY ANDY'S SMILE

Raggedy Andy's smile was gone.

Not entirely, but enough so that it made his face seem onesided.

If one viewed Raggedy Andy from the left side, one could see his smile.

But if one looked at Raggedy Andy from the right side, one could not see his smile. So Raggedy Andy's smile was gone.

It really was not Raggedy Andy's fault.

He felt just as happy and sunny as ever.

And perhaps would not have known the difference had not the other dolls told him he had only one half of his cheery smile left.

Nor was it Marcella's fault. How was she to know that Dickie would feed Raggedy Andy orange juice and take off most of his smile?

And besides taking off one half of Raggedy Andy's smile, the orange juice left a great brown stain upon his face.

Marcella was very sorry when she saw what Dickie had done.

Dickie would have been sorry, too, if he had been more than two years old, but when one is only two years old, he has very few sorrows.

Dickie's only sorrow was that Raggedy Andy was taken from him, and he could not feed Raggedy Andy more orange juice.

Marcella kissed Raggedy Andy more than she did the rest of the dolls that night, when she put them to bed, and this made all the dolls very happy.

It always gave them great pleasure when any of their number was hugged and kissed, for there was not a selfish doll among them.

Marcella hung up a tiny stocking for each of the dollies, and placed a tiny little china dish for each of the penny dolls beside their little spool box bed.

For, as you probably have guessed, it was Christmas eve, and Marcella was in hopes Santa Claus would see the tiny stockings and place something in them for each dollie.

Then when the house was very quiet, the French doll told Raggedy Andy that most of his smile was gone.

"Indeed!" said Raggedy Andy. "I can still feel it! It must be there!"

"Oh, but it really is gone!" Uncle Clem said. "It was the orange juice!"

"Well, I still feel just as happy," said Raggedy Andy, "so let's have a jolly game of some sort! What shall it be?"

"Perhaps we had best try to wash your face!" said practical Raggedy Ann. She always acted as a mother to the other dolls when they were alone.

"It will not do a bit of good!" the French doll told Raggedy Ann, "for I remember I had orange juice spilled upon a nice white frock I had one time, and the stain would never come out!"

"That is too bad!" Henny, the Dutch doll, said. "We shall miss Raggedy Andy's cheery smile when he is looking straight at us!"

"You will have to stand on my right side, when you wish to see my smile!" said Raggedy Andy, with a cheery little chuckle 'way down in his soft cotton inside.

JOHNNY GRUELLE

"But I wish everyone to understand," he went on, "that I am smiling just the same, whether you can see it or not!"

And with this, Raggedy Andy caught hold of Uncle Clem and Henny, and made a dash for the nursery door, followed by all the other dolls.

Raggedy Andy intended jumping down the stairs, head over heels, for he knew that neither he, Uncle Clem nor Henny would break anything by jumping down stairs.

But just as they got almost to the door, they dropped to the floor in a heap, for there, standing watching the whole performance, was a man.

All the dolls fell in different attitudes, for it would never do for them to let a real person see that they could act and talk just like real people.

Raggedy Andy, Uncle Clem and Henny stopped so suddenly they fell over each other and Raggedy Andy, being in the lead and pulling the other two, slid right through the door and stopped at the feet of the man.

A cheery laugh greeted this and a chubby hand reached down and picked up Raggedy Andy and turned him over.

Raggedy Andy looked up into a cheery little round face, with a little red nose and red cheeks, and all framed in white whiskers which looked just like snow.

Then the little round man walked into the nursery and picked up all the dolls and looked at them. He made no noise when he walked, and this was why he had taken the dolls by surprise at the head of the stairs.

The little man with the snow-white whiskers placed all the dolls in a row and from a little case in his pocket he took a tiny bottle and a little brush. He dipped the little brush in the tiny bottle and touched all the dolls' faces with it.

He had purposely saved Raggedy Andy's face until the last. Then, as all the dolls watched, the cheery little white-whiskered man touched Raggedy Andy's face with the magic liquid, and the orange juice stain disappeared, and in its place came Raggedy Andy's rosy cheeks and cheery smile.

And, turning Raggedy Andy so that he could face all the other dolls, the cheery little man showed him that all the other dolls had new rosy cheeks and newly-painted faces. They all looked just like new dollies. Even Susan's cracked head had been made whole.

Henny, the Dutch doll, was so surprised he fell over backward and said, "Squeek!"

When the cheery little man with the white whiskers heard this, he picked Henny up and touched him with the paint brush in the center of the back, just above the place where Henny had the little mechanism which made him say "Mama" when he was new. And when the little man touched Henny and tipped him forward and backward, Henny was just as good as new and said "Mama" very prettily.

Then the little man put something in each of the tiny doll stockings, and something in each of the little china plates for the two penny dolls.

Then, as quietly as he had entered, he left, merely turning at the door and shaking his finger at the dolls in a cheery, mischievous manner.

Raggedy Andy heard him chuckling to himself as he went down the stairs.

Raggedy Andy tiptoed to the door and over to the head of the stairs.

Then he motioned for the other dolls to come.

There, from the head of the stairs, they watched the cheery little white-whiskered man take pretty things from a large sack and place them about the chimneyplace.

"He does not know that we are watching him," the dolls all thought, but when the little man had finished his task, he turned quickly and laughed right up at the dolls, for he had known that they were watching him all the time.

Then, again shaking his finger at them in his cheery manner, the little white-whiskered man swung the sack to his shoulder, and with a whistle such as the wind makes when it plays through the chinks of a window, he was gone—up the chimney.

The dolls were very quiet as they walked back into the nursery and sat down to think it all over, and as they sat there thinking, they heard out in the night the "tinkle, tinkle, tinkle" of tiny sleigh bells, growing fainter and fainter as they disappeared in the distance.

Without a word, but filled with a happy wonder, the dolls climbed into their beds, just as Marcella had left them, and pulled the covers up to their chins.

And Raggedy Andy lay there, his little shoe button eyes looking straight towards the ceiling and smiling a joyful smile—not a "half smile" this time, but a "full size smile."

THE WOODEN HORSE

Santa Claus left a whole lot of toys.

A wooden horse, covered with canton flannel and touched lightly with a paint brush dipped in black paint to give him a dappled gray appearance, was one of the presents.

With the wooden horse came a beautiful red wagon with four yellow wheels. My! The paint was pretty and shiny.

The wooden horse was hitched to the wagon with a patent leather harness; and he, himself, stood proudly upon a red platform running on four little nickel wheels.

It was true that the wooden horse's eyes were as far apart as a camel's and made him look quite like one when viewed from in front, but he had soft leather ears and a silken mane and tail.

He was nice to look upon, was the wooden horse. All the dolls patted him and smoothed his silken mane and felt his shiny patent leather harness the first night they were alone with him in the nursery.

The wooden horse had a queer voice; the dolls could hardly understand him at first, but when his bashfulness wore off, he talked quite plainly.

"It is the first time I have ever tried to talk," he explained when he became acquainted, "and I guess I was talking down in my stomach instead of my head!"

"You will like it here in the nursery very much!" said Raggedy Andy. "We have such jolly times and love each other so much I know you will enjoy your new home!"

"I am sure I shall!" the wooden horse answered. "Where I came from, we—the other horses and myself—just stood silently upon the shelves and looked and looked straight ahead, and never so much as moved our tails."

"See if you can move your tail now!" Henny, the Dutch doll, suggested.

The wooden horse started to roll across the nursery floor and if Raggedy Ann had not been in the way, he might have bumped into the wall. As it was, the wooden horse rolled against Raggedy Ann and upset her but could go no further when his wheels ran against her rag foot.

When the wooden horse upset Raggedy Ann, he stood still until Uncle Clem and Henny and Raggedy Andy lifted him off Raggedy Ann's feet. "Did I frisk my tail?" he asked when Raggedy Ann stood up and smoothed her apron.

"Try it again!" said Raggedy Ann. "I couldn't see!" She laughed her cheery rag doll laugh, for Raggedy Ann, no matter what happened, never lost her temper.

The wooden horse started rolling backward at this and knocked Henny over upon his back, causing him to cry "Mama!" in his squeeky voice.

Uncle Clem, Raggedy Ann, and the tin soldier all held to the wooden horse and managed to stop him just as he was backing out of the nursery door towards the head of the stairs.

Then the dolls pulled the wooden horse back to the center of the room. "It's funny" he said, "that I start moving backward or forward when I try to frisk my tail!"

"I believe it is because you have stood so long upon the shelf without moving," Raggedy Andy suggested. "Suppose you try moving forward!"

Uncle Clem, who was standing in front of the wooden horse, jumped to one side so hastily his feet slipped out from under him, just as if he had been sliding upon slippery ice.

The wooden horse did not start moving forward as Uncle Clem had expected; instead, his silken tail frisked gaily up over his back.

"Whee! There, you frisked your tail!" cried all the dolls as joyfully as if the wooden horse had done something truly wonderful.

"It's easy now!" said the wooden horse. "When I wish to go forward or backward I'll try to frisk my tail and then I'll roll along on my shiny wheels; then when I wish to frisk my tail I'll try to roll forward or backward, like this!" But instead of rolling forward, the wooden horse frisked his tail. "I wanted to frisk my tail then!" he said in surprise. "Now I'll roll forward!" And sure enough, the wooden horse rolled across the nursery floor.

When he started rolling upon his shiny wheels, Raggedy Andy cried, "All aboard!" and, taking a short run, he leaped upon the wooden horse's back. Uncle Clem, Raggedy Ann, Henny, the Dutch doll and Susan, the doll without a head, all scrambled up into the pretty red wagon.

The wooden horse thought this was great fun and round

and round the nursery he circled. His shiny wheels and the pretty yellow wheels of the red wagon creaked so loudly none of the dolls heard the cries of the tiny penny dolls who were too small to climb aboard. Finally, as the wagon load of dolls passed the penny dolls, Raggedy Andy noticed the two little midgets standing together and missing the fun; so, leaning 'way over to one side as the horse swept by them, Raggedy Andy caught both the penny dolls in his strong rag arms and lifted them to a seat upon the broad back of the wooden horse.

"Hooray!" cried all the dolls when they saw Raggedy Andy's feat. "It was just like a Wild West Show!"

"We must all have all the fun we can together!" said Raggedy Andy.

"Good for you!" cried Uncle Clem. "The more fun we can give each other, the more fun each one of us will have!"

The wooden horse made the circle of the nursery a great many times, for it pleased him very much to hear the gay laughter of the dolls and he thought to himself, "How happy I will be, living with such a jolly crowd."

But just as he was about to pass the door, there was a noise upon the stairs and the wooden horse, hearing it, stopped so suddenly Raggedy Andy and the penny dolls went clear over his head and the dolls in the front of the wagon took Raggedy Andy's seat upon the horse's back.

They lay just as they fell, for they did not wish anyone to suspect that they could move or talk.

"Ha! Ha! Ha! I knew you were having a lot of fun!" cried a cheery voice.

At this, all the dolls immediately scrambled back into their former places, for they recognized the voice of the French dollie.

But what was their surprise to see her dressed in a lovely fairy costume, her lovely curls flying out behind, as she ran towards them.

Raggedy Andy was just about to climb upon the horse's

back again when the French doll leaped there herself and, balancing lightly upon one foot, stood in this position while the wooden horse rolled around the nursery as fast as he could go.

Raggedy Andy and the two penny dolls ran after the wagon and, with the assistance of Uncle Clem and Raggedy Ann, climbed up in back.

When the wooden horse finally stopped the dolls all said, "This is the most fun we have had for a *long* time!"

The wooden horse, a thrill of happiness running through his wooden body, cried, "It is the most fun I have *ever* had!"

And the dolls, while they did not tell him so, knew that he had had the most fun because he had given *them* the most pleasure.

For, as you must surely know, they who are the most unselfish are the ones who gain the greatest joy; because they give happiness to others.

JOHNNY GRUELLE

MAKING "ANGELS" IN THE SNOW

"Whee! It's good to be back home again!" said Raggedy Andy to the other dolls, as he stretched his feet out in front of the little toy stove and rubbed his rag hands briskly together, as if to warm them.

All the dolls laughed at Raggedy Andy for doing this, for they knew there had never been a fire in the little toy stove in all the time it had been in the nursery. And that was a long time.

"We are so glad and happy to have you back home again with us!" the dolls told Raggedy Andy. "For we have missed you very, very much!"

"Well," Raggedy Andy replied, as he held his rag hands over the tiny lid of the stove and rubbed them again, "I have missed all of you, too, and wished many times that you had been with me to join in and share in the pleasures and frolics I've had."

And as Raggedy Andy continued to hold his hands over the little stove, Uncle Clem asked him why he did it.

Raggedy Andy smiled and leaned back in his chair. "Really," he said, "I wasn't paying any attention to what I was doing! I've spent so much of my time while I was away drying out my soft cotton stuffing it seems as though it has almost become a habit."

"Were you wet most of the time, Raggedy Andy?" the French doll asked.

"Nearly all the time!" Raggedy Andy replied. "First I would get sopping wet and then I'd freeze!"

"Freeze!" exclaimed all the dolls in one breath.

"Dear me, yes!" Raggedy Andy laughed. "Just see here!" And Raggedy Andy pulled his sleeve up and showed where his rag arm had been mended. "That was quite a rip!" he smiled.

"Dear! Dear! How in the world did it happen? On a nail?" Henny, the Dutch doll, asked as he put his arm about Raggedy Andy.

"Froze!" said Raggedy Andy.

The dolls gathered around Raggedy Andy and examined the rip in his rag arm.

"It's all right now!" he laughed. "But you should have seen me when it happened! I was frozen into one solid cake of ice all the way through, and when Marcella tried to limber up my arm before it had thawed out, it went, 'Pop!' and just bursted.

"Then I was placed in a pan of nice warm water until the icy cotton inside me had melted, and then I was hung up on a line above the kitchen stove, out at Gran'ma's."

"But how did you happen to get so wet and then freeze?" asked Raggedy Ann.

"Out across the road from Gran'ma's home, 'way out in the country, there is a lovely pond," Raggedy Andy explained. "In the summer time pretty flowers grow about the edge, the little green frogs sit upon the pond lilies and beat upon their tiny drums all through the night, and the twinkling stars wink at their reflections in the smooth water. But when Marcella and I went out to Gran'ma's, last week, Gran'ma met us with a sleigh, for the ground was covered with starry snow. The pretty pond was covered with ice, too, and upon the ice was a soft blanket of the white, white snow. It was beautiful!" said Raggedy Andy.

"Gran'ma had a lovely new sled for Marcella, a red one
with shiny runners.

"And after we had visited Gran'ma a while, we went to
the pond for a slide.

"It was heaps of fun, for there was a little hill at one end
of the pond so that when we coasted down, we went scooting
across the pond like an arrow.

"Marcella would turn the sled sideways, just for fun, and
she and I would fall off and go sliding across the ice upon our
backs, leaving a clean path of ice, where we pushed aside the
snow as we slid. Then Marcella showed me how to make
'angels' in the soft snow!"

"Oh, tell us how, Raggedy Andy!" shouted all the dollies.

"It's very easy!" said Raggedy Andy. "Marcella would
lie down upon her back in the snow and put her hands back
up over her head, then she would bring her hands in a circle
down to her sides, like this." And Raggedy Andy lay upon
the floor of the nursery and showed the dollies just how it
was done. "Then," he added, "when she stood up it would
leave the print of her body and legs in the white, white snow,

and where she had swooped her arms there were the 'angel's wings!' "

"It must have looked just like an angel!" said Uncle Clem.

"Indeed it was very pretty!" Raggedy Andy answered. "Then Marcella made a lot of 'angels' by placing me in the snow and working my arms; so you see, what with falling off the sled so much and making so many 'angels,' we both were wet, but I was completely soaked through. My cotton just became soppy and I was ever so much heavier! Then Gran'ma, just as we were having a most delightful time, came to the door and 'Ooh-hooed' to Marcella to come and get a nice new doughnut. So Marcella, thinking to return in a minute, left me lying upon the sled and ran through the snow to Gran'ma's. And there I stayed and stayed until I began to feel stiff and could hear the cotton inside me go, 'Tic! Tic!' as it began to freeze.

"I lay upon the sled until after the sun went down. Two little Chicadees came and sat upon the sled and talked to me in their cute little bird language, and I watched the sky in the west get golden red, then turn into a deep crimson purple and finally a deep blue, as the sun went farther down around the bend of the earth. After it had been dark for some time, I heard someone coming through the snow and could see the yellow light of a lantern. It was Gran'ma.

"She pulled the sled over in back of her house and did not see that I was upon it until she turned to go in the kitchen; then she picked me up and took me inside. 'He's frozen as stiff as a board!' she told Marcella as she handed me to her. Marcella did not say why she had forgotten to come for me, but I found out afterward that it was because she was so wet. Gran'ma made her change her clothes and shoes and stockings and would not permit her to go out and play again.

"Well, anyway," concluded Raggedy Andy, "Marcella tried to limber my arm and, being almost solid ice, it just burst. And that is the way it went all the time we were out at Gran'ma's; I was wet nearly all the time. But I wish you could all have been with me to share in the fun."

And Raggedy Andy again leaned over the little toy stove and rubbed his rag hands briskly together.

Uncle Clem went to the waste paper basket and came back with some scraps of yellow and red paper. Then, taking off one of the tiny lids, he stuffed the paper in part of the way as if the flames were "shooting up!"

Then, as all the dolls' merry laughter rang out, Raggedy Andy stopped rubbing his hands, and catching Raggedy Ann about the waist, he went skipping across the nursery floor with her, whirling so fast neither saw they had gone out through the door until it was too late. For coming to the head of the stairs, they both went head over heels, "blumpity, blump!" over and over, until they wound up, laughing, at the bottom.

"Last one up is a Cocoa baby!" cried Raggedy Ann, as she scrambled to her feet. And with her skirts in her rag hands she went racing up the stairs to where the rest of the dollies stood laughing.

"Hurrah, for Raggedy Ann!" cried Raggedy Andy generously. "She won!"

THE SINGING SHELL

For years and years the beautiful shell had been upon the floor in Gran'ma's front room. It was a large shell with many points upon it. These were coarse and rough, but the shell was most beautiful inside.

Marcella had seen the shell time and time again and often admired its lovely coloring, which could be seen when one looked inside the shell.

So one day, Gran'ma gave the beautiful shell to Marcella to have for her very own, up in the nursery.

"It will be nice to place before the nursery door so the wind will not blow the door to and pinch anyone's fingers!" Gran'ma laughed.

So Marcella brought the shell home and placed it in front of the nursery door. Here the dolls saw it that night, when all the house was still, and stood about it wondering what kind of toy it might be.

"It seems to be nearly all mouth!" said Henny, the Dutch doll. "Perhaps it can talk."

"It has teeth!" the French doll pointed out. "It may bite!"

"I do not believe it will bite," Raggedy Andy mused, as he got down upon his hands and knees and looked up into the shell. "Marcella would not have it up here if it would bite!"

And, saying this, Raggedy Andy put his rag arm into the lovely shell's mouth.

"It doesn't bite! I knew it wouldn't!" he cried. "Just feel how smooth it is inside!"

All the dolls felt and were surprised to find it polished so highly inside, while the outside was so coarse and rough. With the help of Uncle Clem and Henny, Raggedy Andy turned the shell upon its back, so that all the dolls might look in.

The coloring consisted of dainty pinks, creamy whites and pale blues, all running together just as the coloring in an opal runs from one shade into another. Raggedy Andy, stooping over to look further up inside the pretty shell, heard something.

"It's whispering!" he said, as he raised up in surprise.

All the dolls took turns putting their ears to the mouth of the beautiful shell. Yes, truly it whispered, but they could not catch just what it said.

Finally Raggedy Andy suggested that all the dolls lie down upon the floor directly before the shell and keep very quiet.

"If we don't make a sound we may be able to hear what it says!" he explained.

So the dolls lay down, placing themselves flat upon the floor directly in front of the shell and where they could see and admire its beautiful coloring.

Now the dolls could be very, very quiet when they really wished to be, and it was easy for them to hear the faint whispering of the shell.

This is the story the shell told the dolls in the nursery that night:

"A long, long time ago, I lived upon the yellow sand, deep down beneath the blue, blue waters of the ocean. Pretty silken sea weeds grew around my home and reached their waving branches up, up towards the top of the water.

"Through the pretty sea weeds, fishes of pretty colors and shapes darted here and there, playing at their games.

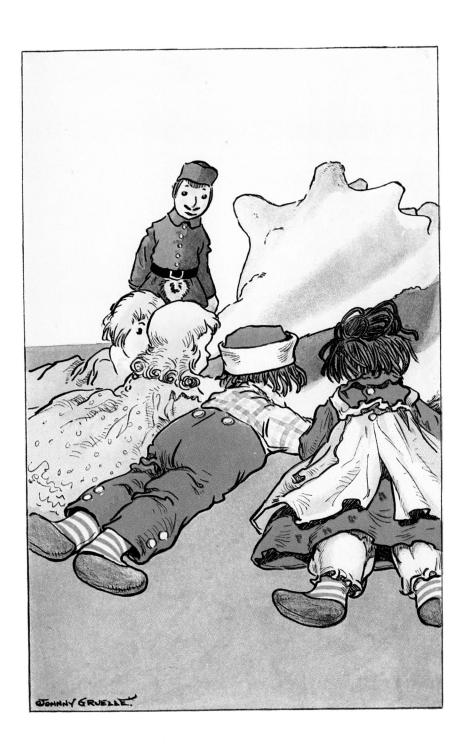

It was still and quiet 'way down where I lived, for even if the ocean roared and pounded itself into an angry mass of tumbling waves up above, this never disturbed the calm waters down where I lived.

"Many times, little fishes or other tiny sea people came and hid within my pretty house when they were being pursued by larger sea creatures. And it always made me very happy to give them this protection.

"They would stay inside until I whispered that the larger creature had gone, then they would leave me and return to their play.

"Pretty little sea horses with slender, curving bodies often went sailing above me, or would come to rest upon my back. It was nice to lie and watch the tiny things curl their little tails about the sea weed and talk together, for the sea horses like one another and are gentle and kind to each other, sharing their food happily and smoothing their little ones with their cunning noses.

"But one day a diver leaped over the side of a boat and came swimming head-first down, down to where I lay. My! How the tiny sea creatures scurried to hide from him. He took me within his hand and, giving his feet a thump upon the yellow sand, rose with me to the surface.

"He poured the water from me, and out came all the little creatures who had been hiding there!"

Raggedy Andy wiggled upon the floor, he was so interested.

"Did the tiny creatures get back into the water safely?" he asked the beautiful shell.

"Oh, yes!" the shell whispered in reply. "The man held me over the side of the boat, so the tiny creatures went safely back into the water!"

"I am so glad!" Raggedy Andy said, with a sigh of relief. "He must have been a kindly man!"

"Yes, indeed!" the beautiful shell replied. "So I was placed along with a lot of other shells in the bottom of the boat and every once in a while another shell was placed amongst us. We whispered together and wondered where we were going. We were finally sold to different people and I have been at Gran'ma's house for a long, long time."

"You lived there when Gran'ma was a little girl, didn't you?" Raggedy Ann asked.

"Yes," replied the shell, "I have lived there ever since Gran'ma was a little girl. She often used to play with me and listen to me sing."

"Raggedy Ann can play 'Peter, Peter, Pumpkin Eater' on the piano, with one hand," said Uncle Clem, "but none of us can sing. Will you sing for us?" he asked the shell.

"I sing all the time," the shell replied, "for I cannot help singing, but my singing is a secret and so is very soft and low. Put your head close to the opening in my shell and listen!"

The dolls took turns doing this, and heard the shell sing softly and very sweetly.

"How strange and far away it sounds!" exclaimed the French doll. "Like fairies singing in the distance! The shell must be singing the songs of the mermaids and the water-fairies!"

"It is queer that anything so rough on the outside could be so pretty within!" said Raggedy Andy. "It must be a great pleasure to be able to sing so sweetly!"

"Indeed it is," replied the beautiful shell, "and I get a great happiness from singing all the time."

"And you will bring lots of pleasure to us, by being so happy!" said Raggedy Andy. "For although you may not enter into our games, we will always know that you are happily singing, and that will make us all happy!"

"I will tell you the secret of my singing," said the shell. "When anyone puts his ear to me and listens, he hears the reflection of his own heart's music, singing; so, you see, while I say that I am singing all the time, in reality I sing only when someone full of happiness hears his own singing as if it were mine."

"How unselfish you are to say this!" said Raggedy Andy. "Now we are ever so much more glad to have you with us. Aren't we?" he asked, turning to the rest of the dolls.

"Yes, indeed!" came the answer from all the dolls, even the tiny penny dolls.

"That is why the shell is so beautiful inside!" said Raggedy Ann. "Those who are unselfish may wear rough clothes, but inside they are always beautiful, just like the shell, and reflect to others the happiness and sunny music within their hearts!"

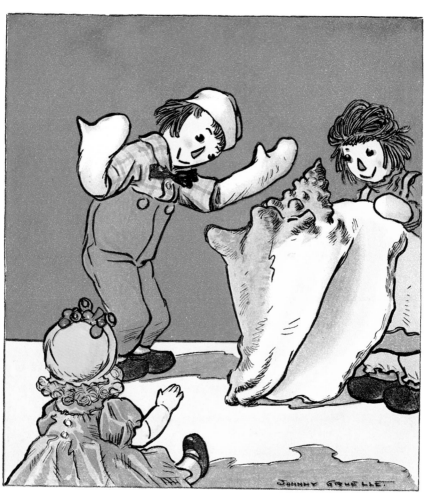

AFTERWORD
Johnny Gruelle and His Beloved Raggedys

"A rich man is one who spends his life in kindness making friends."
—Johnny Gruelle

My grandfather, Johnny Gruelle, lived as he wrote and believed. He was always a child at heart. His books contained nothing to cause fright, glorify mischief, excuse malice, or condone cruelty.

John Barton Gruelle was born Christmas morning, 1880, in Arcola, Illinois, the oldest son of Richard Buckner and Alice Gruelle. Richard, or R.B. as friends called him, was a self-taught landscape painter. When Johnny was two, the family moved to Indianapolis, which was becoming a cultural mecca for artists, writers, and musicians. There the Gruelle family soon became friends with other inspired midwestern artists, and R.B. became a member of the Hoosier Five artist group at this time.

R.B. and Alice saw to it that Johnny and their other children, Prudence and Justin, were exposed to art, literature, and music, and gave them ample opportunities for artistic expression. R. B. allowed the children to experiment freely with the paints and brushes in his home studio, and young Johnny often accompanied his father on landscape painting field trips. No doubt these outings to commune with nature, mixed with lively storytelling and music, instilled in Johnny the power of the written word and a strong appreciation of art for the heart's sake.

In 1903 Johnny was hired as an illustrator for the *Indianapolis Star*. Before long the managing editor recognized Johnny's talent for capturing, in pen and ink, the subtleties and whimsy of everyday life and put Johnny's political cartoons on the *Star*'s front page.

Talent as a cartoonist eventually led Johnny to the *Cleveland Press*. In 1910 at the advice of family and friends, Johnny entered a national competition sponsored by the *New York Herald*, which was seeking a new cartoonist for their Sunday color installment. Johnny's two submissions won first and second place in a blind competition of 1,500 entries. Johnny's first-place entry, "Mr. Twee Deedle" ran for ten years in the *New York Herald*.

Johnny and his wife Myrtle and young daughter, Marcella, relocated to the Norwalk, Connecticut, area. There they built a home for themselves in the Silvermine Artists Colony, not far from Johnny's mother and father, who had moved there earlier.

Using the tried and true techniques of the traditional storyteller, Johnny not only created new, whimsical tales for children, but also created many of the still-prevailing tales about his own life. He also initiated many legends about the genesis of Raggedy Ann and Andy, weaving fanciful details into factual accounts. With the wink of his eye or a flick of his pen, Johnny delighted in transporting all ages to the land of magic and make-believe. This affinity, coupled with his deeply spiritual connection to nature, magic, and all living things, enabled Johnny to create stories and illustrations that are just as loved today as they were when first created.

During 1914–1917 Johnny illustrated a comprehensive edition of Grimms' fairy tales for Cupples and Leon Publishers, and in 1917 wrote and illustrated his own book of original fairy tales, *My Very Own Fairy Stories*, published by P.F. Volland Co. He set many of these tales in a nursery full of dolls, giving each a whimsical name and a personality all its own. One of the dolls—one that would eventually star in her own books of tales—was Raggedy Ann. A doll that he created and patented in 1915, she was Marcella Gruelle's favorite. Around this time Marcella had fallen gravely ill from a contaminated vaccination. Her health slowly deteriorated until her death two years later. Johnny and Myrtle's second-born, Worth (my father), was just four years old at this time. He remembers his big sister with great love, and recollects his mother reading the stories that later became part of the "Raggedy" series of books. Worth's brother Richard was born in 1917 and the first edition of Johnny Gruelle's *Raggedy Ann Stories* was published in 1918. The book was such a hit that Johnny continued to write, illustrate, and have published at least one book a year in the Raggedy Ann and Andy series until his untimely death in 1938.

It is with great pleasure, tradition, and love that I see my grandfather's books back in print again in their original format, to be shared with generations of "Raggedy" lovers past, present, and future.

—Kim Gruelle